WITHDRAWN

D1470068

DATE DUE

The Dog and the Shadow

Will greed bring you more than you already have?

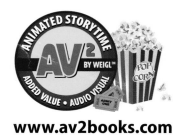

www.av2books.com

Go to **www.av2books.com**, and enter this book's unique code.

BOOK CODE

W 3 5 5 3 1 2

AV² by Weigl brings you media enhanced books that support active learning.

Published by AV² by Weigl
350 5th Avenue, 59th Floor New York, NY 10118

Copyright ©2013 AV² by Weigl
Copyright ©2010 by Kyowon Co., Ltd.

Library of Congress Cataloging-in-Publication Data

The dog and the shadow.
    p. cm. -- (Aesop's fables by AV2)
 Summary: The classic Aesop fable is performed by a troupe of animal actors.
 ISBN 978-1-61913-101-9 (hard cover : alk. paper)
 [1. Fables. 2. Folklore.] I. Aesop.
 PZ8.2.D59 2012
 398.2--dc23
 [E]
                                   2012018703

Printed in the United States in North Mankato, Minnesota
1 2 3 4 5 6 7 8 9 0 16 15 14 13 12

052012
WEP110612

FABLE SYNOPSIS

For thousands of years, parents and teachers have used memorable stories called fables to teach simple moral lessons to children.

In the Aesop's Fables by AV² series, classic fables are given a lighthearted twist. These familiar tales are performed by a troupe of animal players whose endearing personalities bring the stories to life.

In *The Dog and the Shadow*, Aesop and his troupe teach their audience to make the best of what is given to them. They learn not to be greedy, or they will lose what they already have.

This AV² media enhanced book comes alive with...

Animated Video
Watch a custom animated movie.

Try This!
Complete activities and hands on experiments.

Key Words
Study vocabulary and hands-on experiments.

Quiz
Test your knowledge.

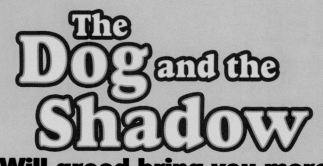

The Dog and the Shadow

Will greed bring you more than you already have?

AV² Storytime Navigation

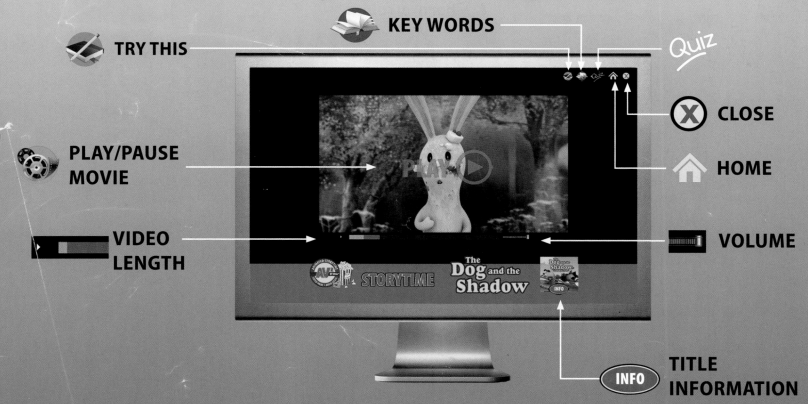

TRY THIS

KEY WORDS

Quiz

CLOSE

HOME

PLAY/PAUSE MOVIE

VIDEO LENGTH

VOLUME

TITLE INFORMATION

INFO

The Players

Aesop
I am the leader of Aesop's Theater, a screenwriter, and an actor.
I can be hot-tempered, but I am also soft and warm-hearted.

Libbit
I am an actor and a prop man.
I think I should have been a lion, but I was born a rabbit.

Presy
I am the manager of Aesop's Theater.
I am also the narrator of the plays.

The Story

One peaceful day, the Shorties were taking a nap in the warmth of the sun.

A pleasant smell was coming from somewhere.

The Shorties quickly jumped to their feet.

"It's snack time. Hurry up, everyone!" Aesop shouted. The Shorties ran to the table, wondering what today's snack would be.

Aesop gave everyone a piece of cake.

"I hope you all enjoy your cake."

Goddard grumbled, "Oink, Oink."

"Everyone's cake is the same size," said Aesop.

"And there is no more cake left."

Goddard begged Aesop for a bigger piece.

Aesop gave Goddard a little piece from his
own plate.

The others began to fuss over their own pieces.

Aesop got angry with them.

"Eat your cake, or I'll eat it all myself."

The Shorties still grumbled, so Aesop

took everyone's cake away.

Then, Aesop hit upon an idea to teach the Shorties a lesson.

He jumped into the carriage and started to write.

After some time, Aesop said to himself,

"Perfect! I wrote just the right play!"

Aesop ran out with his paper in hand.

"Everyone, let's practice the new play!"

15

"This play is called *The Dog and the Shadow*. Let's practice!"

Goddard, who was playing the role of a barking dog, went

across a bridge. He had a loaf of bread in his mouth.

He was too busy eating his bread and did not bark when he

was supposed to!

"You can't bark with food in your mouth!" said Aesop.

Libbit rushed towards Aesop,

"The audience is coming. We have to start the play!"

Aesop looked at Goddard,

"Make sure to bark, and you'll get

your piece of cake back."

Goddard dressed up like a dog,

and the play began.

One spring day, a greedy dog was crossing a bridge with a large piece of bread.

He stopped and looked down into the water.

He thought he saw another dog with a bigger piece of bread.

Goddard did not realize that it was his own shadow in the water.

The greedy dog wanted the other dog's piece of bread.

Goddard tried to bark at the shadow, but he was chewing on the bread. He could not make a sound!

19

Aesop whispered to Goddard.

"Bark! Bark!"

The audience mumbled, "What's the matter with the dog?"

Aesop crawled out and poked Goddard in the ribs.

"Spit it out! Spit it out!"

Goddard dropped his bread in the water.

Goddard tried to save his bread,

but he fell over the edge of the bridge.

Aesop tried to catch Goddard,

but they both fell into the water.

The play was over, and the audience left.

24

"My new play was a mess," said Aesop.

"I hope tonight's dinner will teach us all a lesson."

Presy served the meal.

There were only a few peanuts on each plate.

Goddard looked at the others' plates.

"Don't be greedy again!" said Presy.

Goddard quietly ate his own peanuts.

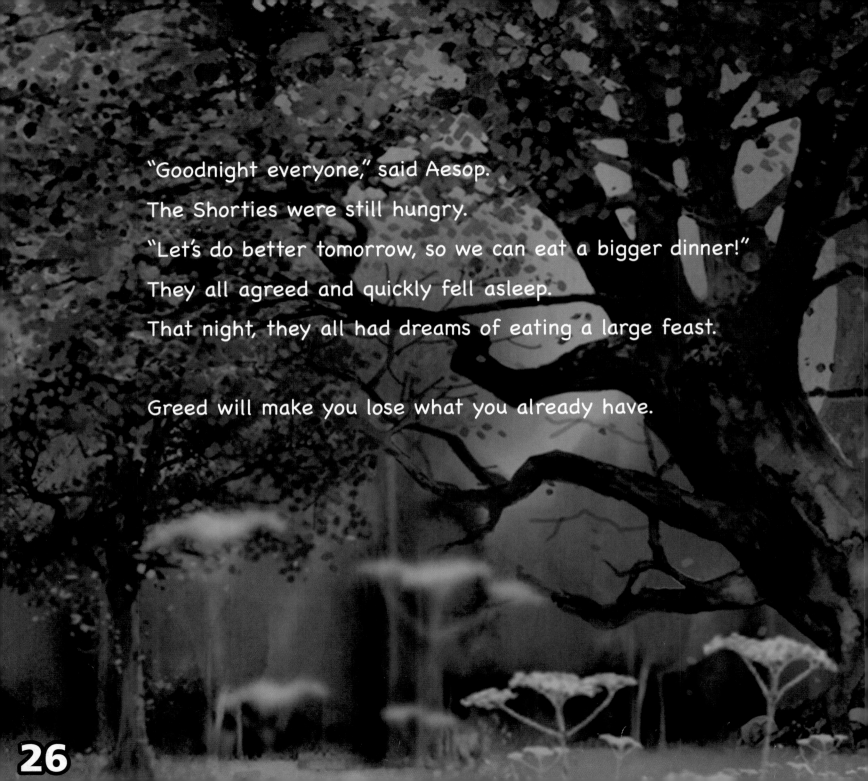

"Goodnight everyone," said Aesop.

The Shorties were still hungry.

"Let's do better tomorrow, so we can eat a bigger dinner!"

They all agreed and quickly fell asleep.

That night, they all had dreams of eating a large feast.

Greed will make you lose what you already have.

What is a Story?

Players

Who is the story about? The characters, or players, are the people, animals, or objects that perform the story. Characters have personality traits that contribute to the story. Readers understand how a character fits into the story by what the character says and does, what others say about the character, and how others treat the character.

Setting

Where and when do the events take place? The setting of a story helps readers visualize where and when the story is taking place. These details help to suggest the mood or atmosphere of the story. A setting is usually presented briefly, but it explains whether the story is taking place in the past, present, or future and in a large or small area.

Plot

What happens in the story? The plot is a story's plan of action. Most plots follow a pattern. They begin with an introduction and progress to the rising action of events. The events lead to a climax, which is the most exciting moment in the story. The resolution is the falling action of events. This section ties up loose ends so that readers are not left with unanswered questions. The story ends with a conclusion that brings the events to a close.

Point of View

Who is telling the story? The story is normally told from the point of view of the narrator, or storyteller. The narrator can be a main character or a less important character in the story. He or she can also be someone who is not in the story but is observing the action. This observer may be impartial or someone who knows the thoughts and feelings of the characters. A story can also be told from different points of view.

Dialogue

What type of conversation occurs in the story? Conversation, or dialogue, helps to show what is happening. It also gives information about the characters. The reader can discover what kinds of people they are by the words they say and how they say them. Writers use dialogue to make stories more interesting. In dialogue, writers imitate the way real people speak, so it is written differently than the rest of the story.

Theme

What is the story's underlying meaning? The theme of a story is the topic, idea, or position that the story presents. It is often a general statement about life. Sometimes, the theme is stated clearly. Other times, it is suggested through hints.

The Dog and the Shadow Quiz

1 What did Aesop give everyone at snack time?

2 Why did Aesop share his cake?

3 What animal did Goddard dress up as in the play?

4 What did Goddard have in his mouth?

5 What did everyone get for dinner?

6 What did the Shorties learn about greed?

Answers:
1. A piece of cake
2. Goddard was being greedy
3. A dog
4. Some bread
5. A few peanuts
6. Greed will make you lose what you already have

Key Words

Research has shown that as much as 65 percent of all written material published in English is made up of 300 words. These 300 words cannot be taught using pictures or learned by sounding them out. They must be recognized by sight. This book contains 113 common sight words to help young readers improve their reading fluency and comprehension. This book also teaches young readers several important content words, such as proper nouns. These words are paired with pictures to aid in learning and improve understanding.

Page	Sight Words First Appearance
4	a, also, am, an, and, be, been, but, can, have, I, of, plays, should, the, think, was
5	always, animals, at, do, food, from, get, good, if, like, never, other, them, to, very, want, with
7	day, feet, one, their, were
9	be, it's, time, up, what, would
10	all, for, his, is, left, more, no, own, said, same, there, you, your
13	away, began, eat, got, he, idea, into, it, or, over, so, started, still, then, took, write
14	after, hand, just, new, out, paper, play, right, some
17	back, did, had, make, not, this, too, we, went, when
19	another, could, down, large, on, saw, sound, thought, water
23	both
25	again, don't, each, few, my, only, us, will
26	night, they

Page	Content Words First Appearance
4	actor, leader, lion, manager, narrator, prop man, rabbit, screenwriter, theater
5	dance, music, pig
7	sun, smell
9	snack, table
10	cake, piece, plate
13	carriage
17	audience, bread, bridge, dog, loaf, mouth, shadow
21	ribs
25	dinner, meal, peanuts, supper
26	dreams

Check out av2books.com for your animated storytime media enhanced book!

1 Go to av2books.com

2 Enter book code W 3 5 5 3 1 2

3 Fuel your imagination online!

www.av2books.com

AV² Storytime Navigation

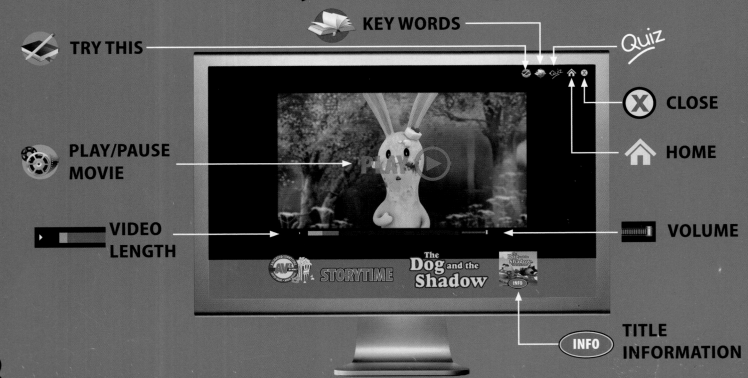

KEY WORDS

TRY THIS

Quiz

X CLOSE

PLAY/PAUSE MOVIE

HOME

VIDEO LENGTH

VOLUME

The Dog and the Shadow

STORYTIME

INFO TITLE INFORMATION